A is for Algorithm
A step by step look
at how to do something,
like read a book.

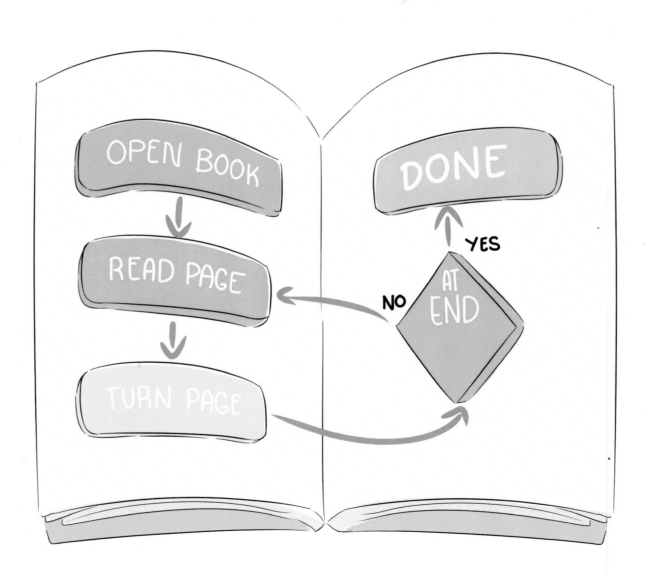

B is for Binary
Just zeroes and ones.
It's how computers say
what works to be done.

C is for Command
It's when you ask.
The computer to do
Some specific task.

D is for Debugging
It can take really long
To figure out
What has gone wrong.

E is for Encryption
So no one can see.
Anything secret
Without the key.

F is for File
How computers store
Pictures and video,
Text and more.

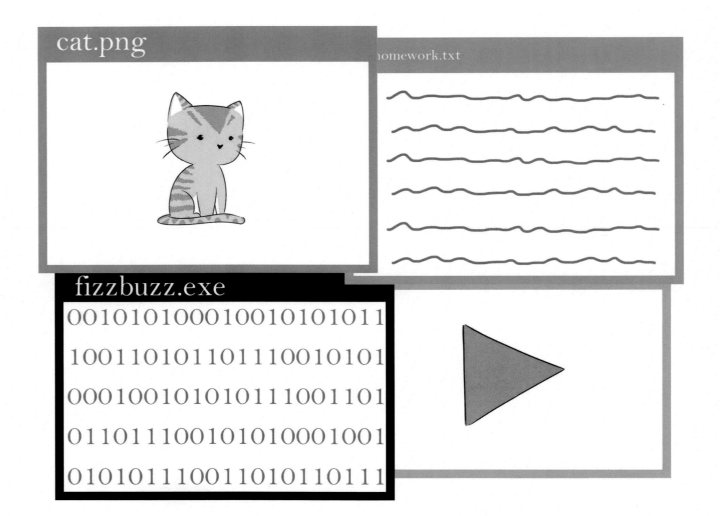

G is for Garbage Collector
when something's no longer needed.
It frees up the memory
so your program is speeded.

H is for Hacker
A word with two meanings
An awesome programmer
or one with bad leanings.

I is for inheritance
Behavior alike
My tabby can do
What any cat might.

J is for Join
Sometimes you'll find
Data's more useful
When it's combined.

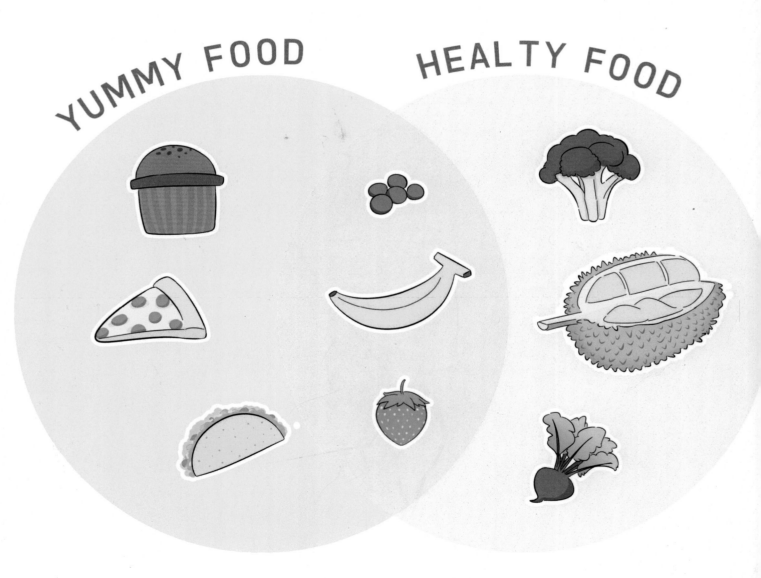

YUMMY FOOD
HEALTY FOOD

K is for Keyboard
All that you need
To type up a program
With skill and speed.

L is for Looping
You take a list.
Do work for each item,
not one is missed.

M is for Map
Lookup and see
What value's associated
With a key.

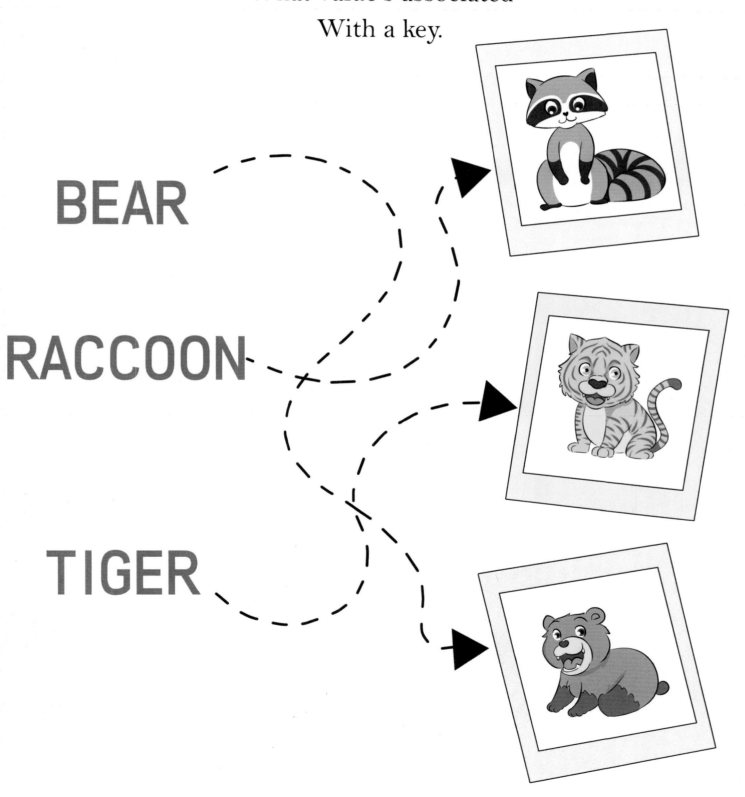

BEAR

RACCOON

TIGER

N is for Null
When you get none.
It can be bad
If you were expecting some.

O is for Open Source.
Share code for all to see
Let others use, copy and change it.
So code can be free.

P is for Program
Coders, they make it!
They debug and fix it,
And sometimes they break it.

Q is for Queueing
People get into line
And get their ice cream
One at a time.

R is for Recursion
It's easy to know
To get the definition
Just trace this arrow.

S is for Source Control
Snapshots of your work.
That shows you what changed
As a nice perk.

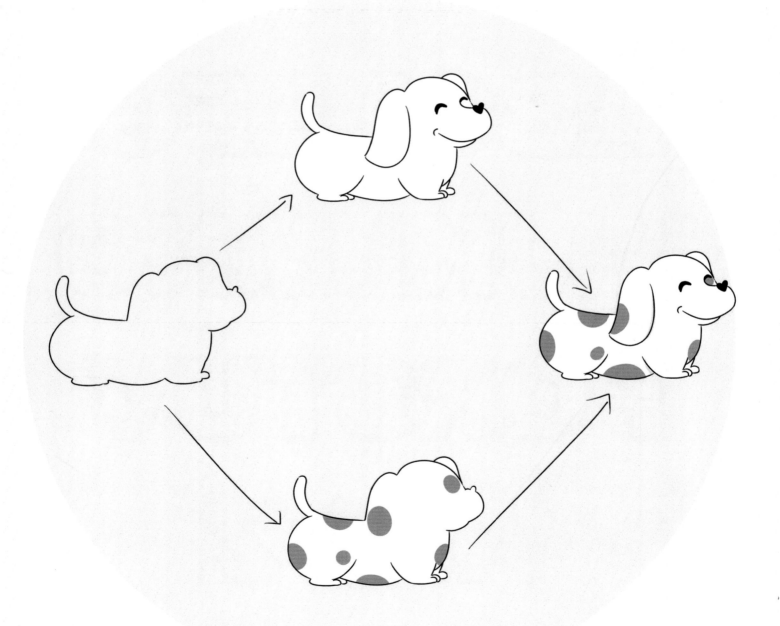

T is for Type
What something can be
A letter is just
A through Z.

ABCDEFG
HIJKLMNO
PQRSTUV
WXYZ

U is for User Interface
How we interact
With computer, phone, and watch
We type, swipe, and tap.

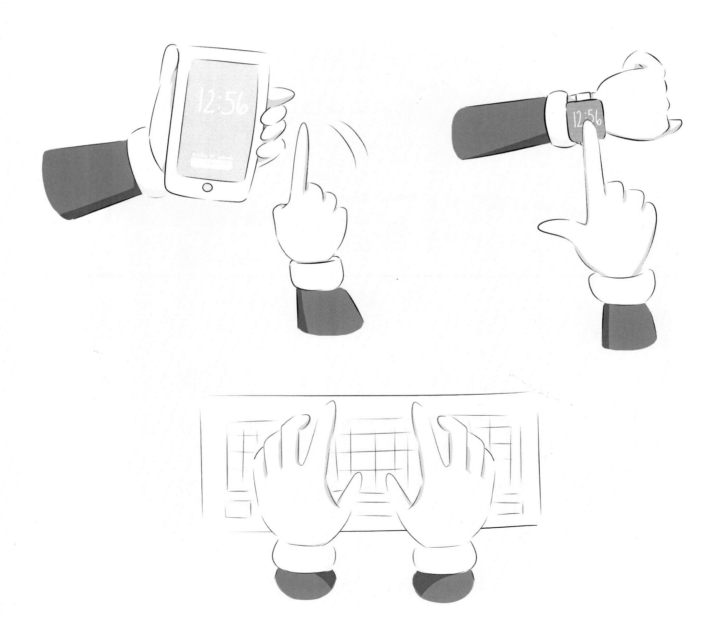

V is for Virtual Machine
It pretends to be
Another computer
Inside your PC.

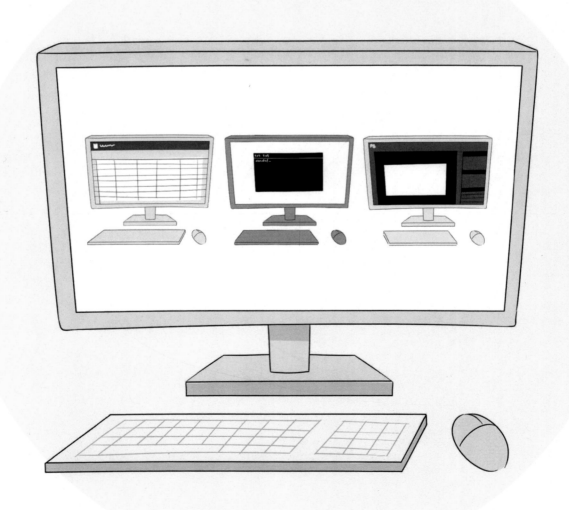

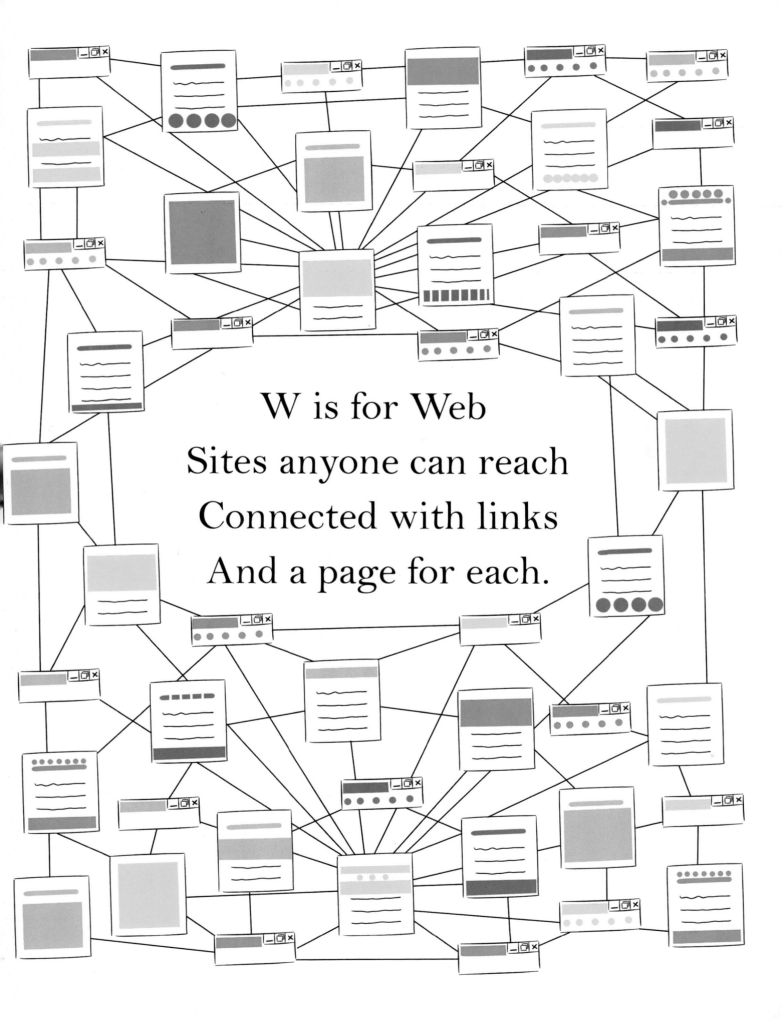

W is for Web
Sites anyone can reach
Connected with links
And a page for each.

X is for Xor
One is all you can take
Like when you have to choose
Between cookies OR cake.

Y is for Yak Shaving
Work that seems unconnected.
But simplifies everything
So your work is affected.

"Once I finish shaving the yak I can
ride over the mountain.
But the yak can't cross the river
so I'll trade him to the
ferry boat captain.
But I need his fur to make
a coat to...."

Z is for Zipping
When lists are combined
So that items are grouped
By how they're aligned.

Made in the USA
San Bernardino, CA
27 August 2017